to the Flag of the
United States of
America, and to the
Republic for which it
stands, one nation
under God, indivisible,
with liberty and
justice for all.

DARIA PEOPLES-RILEY

AMERICA
My Love
AMERICA
My Heart

Greenwillow Books
An Imprint of HarperCollins*Publishers*

For Jordan and Cameron—D. P-R.

Through all these things, you are more
than conquerors through him who loved us.
—Romans 8:37

America, My Love, America, My Heart

Manufactured in Italy. For information address HarperCollins Children's Books,
a division of HarperCollins Publishers, 195 Broadway, New York, NY 10007.
www.harpercollinschildrens.com

The full-color art was created with oil paint and graphite on paper.
The text type is American Garamond BT.

Library of Congress Cataloging-in-Publication Data

Names: Peoples-Riley, Daria, author, illustrator.
Title: America, my love, America, my heart / Daria Peoples-Riley.
Description: First edition. | New York, NY : Greenwillow Books, an imprint of HarperCollinsPublishers, [2021] |
Audience: Ages 4-8. | Audience: Grades 2-3. | Summary: "America, do you love me? A single question from a single child multiplies across the country with every page turn, inviting in more and more children of color—and their questions"—Provided by publisher. Includes author's note about growing up as a brown girl, whose grandmother and great-grandmother spoke Louisiana Creole, reciting the Pledge of Allegiance with her class every morning.
Identifiers: LCCN 2020035392 | ISBN 9780062993298 (hardcover)
Subjects: CYAC: Self-esteem—Fiction. | African Americans—Fiction. | Patriotism—Fiction.
Classification: LCC PZ7.1.P44738 Ame 2021 | DDC [E]—dc23
LC record available at https://lccn.loc.gov/2020035392

21 22 23 24 25 RTLO 10 9 8 7 6 5 4 3 2 1
First Edition

 Greenwillow Books

America, *the Brave*.

America, *the Bold*.

America *to Have*.

America *to Hold*.

America, *My Country.*

Do you love me?

Do you love me from the inside out?
Do you love me from the outside in?

Do you love the way I speak?
In English? Yes?
Spanish? No?
And in *my* Creole?

Do you love mi fuerza?
Mô batay?

The way my fists clench against my hips?
The way my legs stretch strong?

Do you love mi historia?

Mô vwayaj?

From shore to shore?

East to West?

South to North?

From then to now?

From there to here?

Where my glory rises
in the belly of my soul?

Where I swing my halo to and fro?

Where I am loved?
Where I am whole?

Do you love me when I raise my hand?

My head?

My voice?

When I whisper?
When I SHOUT?

Do you love me when I stand?

Stand in?
Stand up?
Stand out?

Do you love my yes?
Do you love my no?

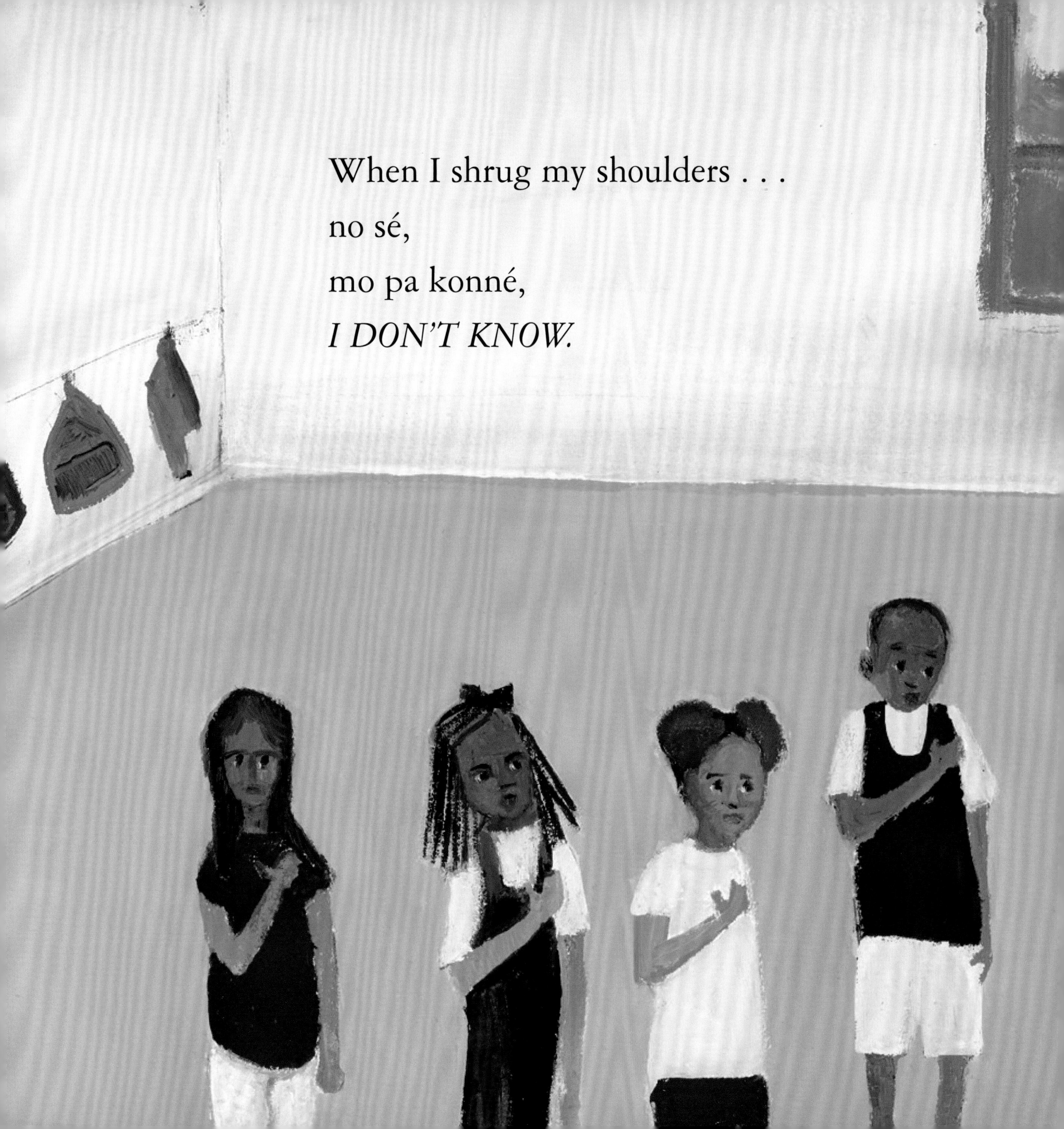

When I shrug my shoulders . . .
no sé,
mo pa konné,
I DON'T KNOW.

How long will it be,
how long will it take.

How long must I wait . . .

for you to love me

from sea to shining sea.

America, *mi amor*.

America, *mô kè*.

Do you love my black?

Do you love my brown?

Do you love my throne?

Do you love my crown?

Do you love my brave?
Do you love my bold?

Am I to have?
Am I to hold?

America, *Land of the Free*.
America, *'Tis of Thee*.

America, *I am you*.

America, *you are me*.

AUTHOR'S NOTE

Like many children of color, I often experienced racism and biases at school. Back then, I didn't know the words to describe how I was treated, but I do remember feeling as though my classmates and my teachers liked one another more than they liked me. My experiences caused me to question many things about myself.

Sometimes I wondered if they treated me differently because my family was black and theirs weren't. Or because my family was different from the other families in my community. My grandmother and great-grandmother spoke a different language. We ate foods others didn't eat, like red beans and rice and gumbo. Unfortunately, I often changed who I was to fit in. I also pretended that the way I was treated didn't bother me. But it did. It broke my heart.

Every morning our class recited the Pledge of Allegiance. It was a time to be quiet, to reflect. But as the only brown girl in most of my classes, I didn't feel free to be myself in my school, in my classroom, or with my teachers and classmates. My country, America, didn't feel free to me.

I wrote this book because maybe you feel the same way sometimes. And I never want you to make my mistake and feel like you have to change any part of who you are, to fit in with people who don't love *all* of you.

Those people are the ones who need to change. It is their responsibility to learn how to love all of you better—your skin color, your language, your culture, your religion, and anything else that makes you different from them. And the best way you can help them is to always be yourself. You are not wrong to be you.

Louisiana Creole and Spanish Language

My great-grandmother and grandmother learned to speak Louisiana Creole in New Roads, Louisiana—one of the few regions where people speak the language. Louisiana Creole is one type of French Creole. Most of its speakers are descendants of slaves. It is often described as a language spoken by the uneducated, because it is different from the French we learn in school. Today, Louisiana Creole is an endangered language. Many languages spoken by people of color are no longer in existence, but Granmá and Nana retained their first language by speaking with family and friends.

As a young girl, I was fascinated by Nana's ability to navigate language. She spoke Louisiana Creole with Granmá, exchanged Spanish greetings with friends and neighbors, and enjoyed sharing her rich culture with us. Unfortunately, I speak only English, but I now have the opportunity to celebrate her love for languages.

My hope is that this book will inspire you to retain, reclaim, and revitalize all of who you are, and most importantly, to write and tell your historia.

(Left) The author with her great-grandmother, Leona Duplessis (Granmá).
(Right) Leona Duplessis and the author's grandmother, Josephine Duplessis (Nana).

(Left) The author with Leona Duplessis.
(Right) The author with Josephine Duplessis.